A Bright and Borrowed Light

A Bright and Borrowed Light

POEMS

Courtney Kampa

WILLIAM MORROW
An Imprint of HarperCollins*Publishers*

Some material was previously published in another format. *Our Lady of Not Asking Why* © 2017.

Without limiting the exclusive rights of any author, contributor or the publisher of this publication, any unauthorized use of this publication to train generative artificial intelligence (AI) technologies is expressly prohibited. HarperCollins also exercise their rights under Article 4(3) of the Digital Single Market Directive 2019/790 and expressly reserve this publication from the text and data mining exception.

This is a work of fiction. Names, characters, places, and incidents are products of the author's imagination or are used fictitiously and are not to be construed as real. Any resemblance to actual events, locales, organizations, or persons, living or dead, is entirely coincidental.

A BRIGHT AND BORROWED LIGHT. Copyright © 2025 by Will Anderson Music LLC. All rights reserved. No part of this book may be used or reproduced in any manner whatsoever without written permission except in the case of brief quotations embodied in critical articles and reviews. For information, address HarperCollins Publishers, 195 Broadway, New York, NY 10007. In Europe, HarperCollins Publishers, Macken House, 39/40 Mayor Street Upper, Dublin 1, D01 C9W8, Ireland.

HarperCollins books may be purchased for educational, business, or sales promotional use. For information, please email the Special Markets Department at SPsales@harpercollins.com.

harpercollins.com

FIRST EDITION

Library of Congress Cataloging-in-Publication Data has been applied for.

ISBN 978-0-06-342945-1

Printed in the United States of America

25 26 27 28 29 LBC 5 4 3 2 1

CONTENTS

1

Take Me with You	11
The Law of Large Numbers	12
After Balthus	14
Cherry Preserves	15
Credo	16
Driving into the Lilacs	17
Ars Balletica	18

2

Self-Portrait by Someone Else	23
Baby Love	24
The Cool Kids	27
Short Essay at the Sink	28
Short Essay on Devotion	29
Edelweiss	30

3

Saint Anthony and the Jarflies	35
Sister	39
War of the Roses	40
Mercy	41
Replica	42

4

Regarding the Woman Lying Naked in the Grass	45
The Rules	46
Miscarriage	48

Fifth Joyful Mystery	50
Cardiac	51
Piccola Morte	53

5

Annunciation	57
Wax Wings	59
Sinfonietta	60
Pink Moon	61
Letter to His Wife	62
Refrain of Him Singing Songs with Her about Us	64
Little Dogs	65

6

Eyelash	69
How to Make Love in a Poem	71
Nocturne in What Now Feels Like a Very Silly Dress	74
Cartography	75
At Their Wedding	77
Skin and Other Weapons	79

7

Inventory of Half-Burnt Offerings	83
Fabric	85
Black Licorice	86
Errata	87
Elegy at Middle River	88
It's You I Like	90
A Note from Will Anderson, Courtney's Husband	95
Notes	99
Acknowledgments	101

A Bright and Borrowed Light

*Like a bell shaken from someone's hands
I also gleam, with as much of noon as I can take
anointed with a bright and borrowed light.*

Take Me with You

Put your ribs into the wind when you say it.
Expose a pearl-bellied throat to the sky.
So many words for wrapping your mind around
the self, instead of your arms around the ankles
of another. *Take me with you.* Say it, and feel
that ache in the teeth, the one unlearned
as a child, when, in a snap for sweetness, you bit
front-teeth-first into ice cream. No, much better
to use the tongue like a spoon, or a thorn. Safer
to claim and puncture by approaching from the side.
Better to say *I'll come along too*, or *hey cool, I'm walking
that direction anyway*, but never *take me with you*. Never
to show the heart so translucent and clear—an orb
of glass, burned and blown thin enough to shatter.
So much talk of abandon, but all along *here* is where
the word was pointing: the airy pause before an answer,
bones humming like a struck gong. Your pulse's
trembling, pale and light, as the dusted wings of a moth;
as a milky circle of sea-foam on the beach,
the water rising ever closer to the spot where you
delicately, desperately sway.

The Law of Large Numbers

A man sits across from me, patterned silk padlock
at his neck, and orders us whatever
people drink from flutes at brunch and talks
about his theory that *tenderness* and *paying
attention to things* are synonyms
but he does not look at me
when he says it. I also have a theory
that in the lighting of certain restaurants
the law stating rarities occur within certain spans
of time simply because crazier things
have happened, shifts from hope
to a source of paranoia. This city is as large
as its exceptions. This city is one dead pigeon
from its knees. I don't know what
I'd have said yesterday had I spoken
to the girl on the other side of the blood stain
on the A-C-E platform, who seemed sad or
was maybe just waiting, while all the supernaturally
common things that happen between people
went on above our heads. I am slowly unlearning
my own story. I am slowly surer
people introduce us to ourselves. I'm bored
by math but read somewhere the velocity
at which one body turns from another
is the same speed it takes the soul to fold
in upon itself, a number star-hard
and constant, dividing evenly

into the wattage required to light a ribcage
from within for eight seconds, or the length
of time it takes standard-size pearls to melt
in vinegar. What sort of person melts
a pearl. What sort of person goes as long as I do
without touch. For two weeks now
a man's been squatting at the corner of my street,
shaping a Madonna with moon-colored shards
from plaster and broken tile.
He uses both hands, fits a jagged bolt of glass
into her hip. He says he smashed the pieces
himself, and he does not look at her
when he says it. Then says it again. Dizzy mockingbird
doubling its own exquisite sound.

After Balthus

What moves is dying, and what is dying
must make due with less. And still, a sudden pathos
of half breath, this air's frayed-syllables, bleached gold
in the city's afterrain. Still this wick-wet road, this wax.
And so the unscrubbed faces of the windows
look inward; so the door's hinge cries a pitch higher
when opened out. So the streetlight's gray bells
peal in their relentless sooty glow. So,
in the avenue's shadow, we'll weigh all that is taken
against what we must hand back.

Cherry Preserves

I had been working all day on a jigsaw
and was frustrated with the thickness of my fingers.
I was frustrated with everything, but especially
with my fingers and how they swell up at the times
I need them most delicate. When the phone rang
I picked up, and a woman with a voice like raspberries
said, "James?" and I said, "Hello?" and she said again,
"James? It's Inga." I am not James, but I *am* a man
with a weakness for the name Inga. "Hello Inga," I said.
"I'm at the grocery, is there anything we need?" she asked.
I got up from my chair to the cupboard. "Grapefruits,"
I said. "Anything else?" she asked. "Cherry preserves."
Because of her voice I could think of nothing
but fruit. "You don't like cherry preserves, James,"
Inga said. "Well, Inga, I've been a fool," I said. Then
I told her how sorry I was for being a fool, and I'm
pretty sure I meant it. The line went silent. Even her tin
grocery cart stopped trembling around in the background.
I heard her sniffle, and she told me when she got home
she would slip into her silky nightie with the slit and bake
those Martha Stewart sugar cookies I loved so much.
I said thank you and hung up, and waited for the knock
of my cherry preserves at the door. I was hungry.
I was thick-fingered and knew that somewhere in the world
there was a batch of cookies burning.

Credo

No finer thing can happen
to walls in a kitchen

than to seem this fraught
with light, the two

of us within them
growing suddenly aware

of being outnumbered
by the spoons.

Driving into the Lilacs

Like anything, it had traveled a distance
to get there. Careening, coming to a stop, cradled absurdly
in the tight, reddish buds. Then, as if learning something new
about itself, it kept very still.
And like anything nightgowned, for a first time,
in purple, it liked it
                        and got comfortable.
Like anything indefatigable, it was not. The wheels were tired
of being wheels. And as could be expected, the flowers had grown
so thick in their beauty they needed to be shaken
to feel anything. The white branches
freaked, arranged
                    across the windshield like wilis
in the dark. What was crushed grew more fragrant
then dropped. The roots strained
to *stay* roots. Leaves deepened the headlights until its lacquer
nearly pearled. *Sort of amazing*,
someone decided. And someone else agreed.

Ars Balletica

It sits in the slow burn
of its own feathers. It dreams easy. And leaps. And fails
to mention to the rest of us what could happen
if it keeps happening—keeps leaving itself
in sun-spots the way people do
their shoes along the stairs. It mixes
red wine with rum and soon
regrets it. It regrets nothing. Its one wish
is to bear a more-exact resemblance
to itself, well-lit and from the proper distance,
transforming on command like a fist
when you open your hand. It hides
its teeth, which have not been tried
and found wanting, but found difficult and left
untried. It flies
because it takes itself lightly. It's dragged like the bones
of our bodies over every awful kind
of love. And it's proud to be alive like that, dying
from another. It wakes the dead
vegetables from our crisper, cucumbers re-greening
all at once. It scrubs the dishes before it breaks
them, which makes no sense. *It* makes
no sense. It is the dissatisfying sparkle
of pond-life, and the pond-life, also. It's the smell
of a barn on fire but doesn't like it
if you say so. It's the vacant space where *already* and *ever*

are never not looking at each other. It wants to want
for nothing, which it does, but also wants
a purpose, which it has already, which is just to hold itself
together. Beauty is what the soul has made
suffice. No one has ever seen God.

*I will never untangle my hair
from almost half your life.*

Self-Portrait by Someone Else

The afternoon we traced our second grade bodies
with poster paint, legs V-shaped on paper
like the outlines of victims at a crime scene,
I was the only girl stuck partnered with a boy—
his knuckles filthy from prying back scalps
of onion grass, bug shells crushed up in his teeth
because he'd liked the sound. He refused
all paint-colors but blue. Leaned over me,
complaining loudly to his friends. Then his lip,
heavy with focus. And the red wing
of his tongue. Dragging his paintbrush
like a match in a room of gasoline. The week before
Debbie Kaw passed a note saying babies
came from standing too close to a boy,
or if one sweat on you, or spat
in your direction. So the girls called it brave, what I did,
letting one trace me. And I let them think so—
let them run ahead in the carpool line,
the blood still returning to my knees.
Let my mother hang it full length on the refrigerator.
The white space something I'd stepped from.
Its thick blue line sort of wobbly
between my thighs, where his hands shook.
In the mornings my little sister would stand
on one foot, looking at it. Her groggy pajamas.
Her hands playing in her hair.

Baby Love

Gregory had a mole below his left eye
and sometimes kids in our fifth grade class
would tease him, saying he had chocolate
on his face. I was the girl who knew it
was his left eye and not his right. Who listened
in secret to *Oldies 100*—music like "Baby Love" by the Supremes
and knew every Patsy Cline song by heart. Gregory
didn't backpack pocket blades to school like Richard
or look up girls' skirts beneath the monkey bars
the way Kenny did, whose mom let him watch
all the Late Night TV he wanted. He was nothing
like Vinny who'd steal the grape juice box
off your desk when you weren't looking.
And he didn't mock William, whose dad worked hard
for a gasoline company—gasoline has the word gas
in it, which all the cool kids thought
was *pretty funny; really classic.* Gregory had immaculate
Ticonderoga erasers and he made my knee-socks droop
and he made my weak bony ankles
weaker. At recess before summer, a soft piece of sidewalk
tar was thrown at my feet and I looked up
and there he was, skipping backwards, a rocket wanting
me to chase him. Mrs. Rivers led him off to suggest
alternative ways of procuring
female attention and in those awful green uniform pants
he looked back at me and winked—which is not
something the average fifth grader does

to another fifth grader. Three weeks later his winking face was fed
into the teeth of a triple car wreck. Eleven years
and I'm still mouthing the triple syllables
of his name. Not because he needs me to
but because I have no alternative way of procuring
his attention. At school I quit talking, Colin inches
from my face taunting SAY-SOME-THING
but I didn't, so now I *will* say something, I will say
that I cried at our class talent show, watching Gregory's mom
out in the audience, shirt misbuttoned, camera readied,
looking for him, and seeing him
nowhere. I will say that with Gregory gone there was no one
to stop the boys from snapping
Stephen's stutter like a twig across their knees. I'll say ours
was a misfit purity. That after art he gave me
his scissors and I swapped
him mine, both blades aimed forward, looking at each other
like we'd just done something
dangerous. Handles inked with initials
in handwriting not his, marked the way mothers mark us carefully
when we walk into the world. I'll say that I still
have them. Gregory, ask me to name a thing
as indestructibly beautiful as you, and I cannot. Time disfigures
those who breathe and those of us who no longer can
but none of that has touched you. Not the cruelty
of children. Not the gravel and glass
that pushed their way into your green
restless legs. Not the ugliness of an ambulance
come too late. Not the small grass square

that mothers and quilts you. Not even the skid marks
below your brother's eyes, tire treads
red across his chest. Love is nothing
if not what takes its time. It takes sweet
time and it's taken eleven years of not trusting
the pitch of my voice or the shamed
insufficiency of what I have
to say—that at your service I got no further
than taking a holy card from the altar boy; picture
of an angel as dark-haired as you: an angel I'd soon shred
to ribbons, my hand around those handles for the first
and only time. Gregory, think of me
in St. Joe's parking lot in July in a sweaty cotton skirt.
Think of my confession to that angel, in his headband
of light, how much I liked
you too. Hoping you had stopped a moment
in the beatific beating of your wings—in the now-familiar strumming
of that strange, beseeching harp.

The Cool Kids

invited me along as far as the pasture gate
where they'd meet to smoke and crunch cans.
Each girl with the waist of a yellow jacket
and the boys sharp with desire
to sting. They were going cow tipping.
At the blackboard a week before,
Mr. Shuster had said sometimes "to love"
means "to push," but this was taking things too far.
We saw her sleeping alone
her espresso spots so beautiful I was sure
we wouldn't go through with it.
Maybe we needed a second cow to compare her to.
Her ribs cracked against the ground
in a noise you wouldn't let yourself hear twice.
Four hooves kicking, helpless, udder askew.
They called her Galileo, the star-stunned outcast.
"A grazer *and* a gazer!" someone said. *Pretty funny—really classic.*
The cow thrashing starward like a beetle.
I stood there slack-jawed at the foam
and ferment. I wondered if this is what it feels like
to be pinned down by the sky. If the sensation around my ankles
had something to do with being tangled
in my own shadow. And the cow,
disrobed like a maple in the fall, her spots crushed
velvet, warm against the grass. Closed-up and famished,
holding whatever the hell we need most
an arm's length from the chest.

Short Essay at the Sink

"If you're not gonna tell her, I am.
If you're gonna sit there smiling
while our little girl brings home a clown
like that. I don't like this at all, I got
a real bad smell off that guy.
Don't act like you didn't notice how
he peeled that orange. I've never seen
anyone so confused by a piece of fruit.
Acting like you handed him a Rubik's Cube
to snack on. Good God, Kate. No,
I'm serious. You want grandkids? If you
think that guy's gonna give you
grandkids, you're crazy. I'll be nice
about it, don't worry, I'll be a goddamn
poet—I just gotta pull her aside
and remind her people die all the time
without ever knowing simple things
about themselves. She'll get what I mean."

Short Essay on Devotion

"What people say about their mothers
is true, but then it isn't. And
what they don't say about mothers
with sons and no daughters is also true
and that's why nobody
says it. The woman spent twenty years
washing her nightgowns with our jockstraps
and somehow still speaks
to us. She must be a saint, not to mention
she probably actually is one—puts on a veil
in church, the whole deal. The big family joke
was that she was always sneaking off
to christen the neighbor's baby
in the bathroom sink, only it wasn't a joke,
that actually happened. When we went to college
she'd give us these clear plastic baggies
with blessed salt—to like, sprinkle around
our dorms or whatever, and it looked *just*
like cocaine. Tom and I'd call it 'the crack pack'
but she never caught on. Pretty sure
she still thinks I've never
heard of drugs. You'll love her. Actually,
babe you should maybe, I dunno, button up
your shirt a little higher—we're almost here."

Edelweiss

> *"how to make friends"*—

—is an internet search my little sister made
last night according to our family's Mac OS X's

recent history, along with "what to say" and "what to say to kids"
and "what to say to kids who are popular"

to which Google responded: *Did you mean: what to **try** to say
to kids who are popular?* offering mapped directions

to the local middle schools. The manufacturer's instructions
of her old crib once cautioned body-weights

over sixty pounds, but I remember, at twelve, climbing into it
with her in the middle of the night—filled, also, with the sounds

my mother used to make, singing "Edelweiss": those highest notes
of impossible, Austrian accuracy,

so pitchy they made me feel, for a moment, her helplessness.
Ordinarily, I would not have ended that thought

there; I'd have tried to take it somewhere
take-able, but that was really all I felt: the armless vertigo

in the height of a note you can't reach, a cracking only angels
and insects can hear. The wondering is-there-something-fixable-

inside-of-me. Tune of *bloom and grow, bloom and grow*,
which, I'm much surer now, happens only in reverse.

*Your body, which is
like my body, so I already
know how it ends.*

Saint Anthony and the Jarflies

    I.

My sister just did that thing with the left corner
of her mouth that means she's thirsty, or our dad

said something to her
using very few words, or the cabinet under the stove is open
and the vanilla gone, or she just saw our baby sister at the edge

of the diving board in her oversized t-shirt,
holding our new black puppy out
        over the deep end—its tail wrapped
around a hind leg, wetting itself, and her, laughing

like a glass cup dropped from our hands.

II.

It's my job to water the vegetables by the pool
       and it's July, the plants frozen

with heat, the jarflies that waited seven years for today
crawling back in their holes.
                    In this weather even the present feels
like a memory: I was squatting
at the chlorinated water, filling a pitcher by its throat.
I recalled the feeling
             of keeping something alive.
Was moved, for a moment, at how unmoved I was
by our eggplant shriveling to shapes of carrots. There was daylight
              more often than not—the moon nothing
but its own thin-hot scar in the sky.

III.

Our baby sister says she can't find her swimsuits—
                     all nine of them—prays
to Saint Anthony, patron of what's missing, or lost,
      and she looks again where she's looked before,

same chest of drawers, same shoeboxes
under her bed. I remember a summer I caught
daddy longlegs with my middle sister—
                                  how she'd held their tick-bodies
between a finger and thumb as her other hand

pulled: asking of their eight limbs if they loved her,
      loved her not—

IV.

and it was like that. How last week I swam laps
    until the current-less water slapped

at the concrete sides. How my sister stood dragging her foot
    across the surface like a mosquito. How I was wishing

I'd touch her face when I talked to her. I kept
    meaning to. Our azaleas had reached

their most basic and unadorned, so green
we couldn't find where they ended and the spade-tipped choke

    of Virginia Creeper began. How there is nothing like
beauty. And there was nothing we did to save them.

Sister

A tongue the color of strawberry yogurt,
the horse takes my—no wait, my *sister's*—
rough, wooly sweater into its mouth
like a palmful of oats. In that old photograph,
thirteen-year-old skin chapped
by the downwind gust of adolescence,
my mouth stretches to a sudden, lemon-like hoop,
half in shock at that thick, wet touch,
the other in alarm, in thinking I was done for—
the clothing smuggled from her closet
now encrusted with the cement of horse spit
and carrot paste. My blue eyes already conniving
a plan to ensure that the deep green in hers
never know. That night, while she slept,
I would fix this: pick my way across her cluttered
floor, soundless as a deer over the husks
of dried leaves—a sister knowing nothing so well
as how to borrow the things she should not.

War of the Roses

    after Richard Siken

Two of us compare the greatness of our lives, measuring the size
of the hands of the men
                        we are about to marry. Love, sister, is not freedom
        from the touch of other loves. My voice disappearing
into your name. Your name disappearing in his voice.
                Love, sister, is a clarity
                              that resembles injury
        and is too difficult for both of us. Outside, our mother's
picking beetles off her roses—they bob like empty pennies
        in their plastic cup. Blooms tied-together at the wrists, all kith,
                all bloodlet. Inside, our mother's
blue Britannicas would call this the traditionally concave architecture
of tenderness: bottomless
                    until it isn't. Would call it piecrust,
                        or sharing sweaters, or the dumb hunger
            of pianos. This love, sister, we hold
    like household scissors
               against each other's throats. Nothing human in you
is alien to me. And you—you know by now
                            what I'm made from.

Mercy

was the game we played, squeezing hands
during the *Our Father*
at 10:30 Mass. The winner: whoever hurt longest
in silence. Only the small muscles
of sisters. The brittle glow
of her hair, its morning smell of butter
and eggs. Glasses hooked around my ears, lenses
thick as Oreos. Learning compassion
must be begged for. But what we knew
of begging was singing
orphans in musicals. And all I knew of need
was the dollar Richard Barry gave me
to tell people I was his girlfriend,
folded in my pocket though the collection basket
had passed. All I grasped of her hands
at that age was their color: green-white,
sticky, bruised. Like squeezing a pear.
Our bodies bent over the pew, driven to sound
but kept quiet. Call it ruthless, or resistless.
Blame it on the edges of our playground,
where gentleness was just a lack
of something stronger. Or the way *deliver us*
sounded in Latin. I thought belief could
be touched, her pulse quickening in my hands.
I have not forgotten what it looked like.

Replica

Hip beside hip in the same bed, our window opened
                            to a dark Virginia rain. Her ankles sticky

like they always are, our yellow hair
                      splayed like a half-threshed field, both kept awake
        by the sound of the other
feigning sleep. Even in the dark, pretending to possess
            what we suspect the other has. Static's blue jump

between our sleeves. Before bed we'd stood barefoot and thirsty,
                    the stovetop aching its orange rings. Two faces

scrubbed bright and raw. Which of us is knee-deep
                  in the other? Which is more than just one?

A kitchen swept of its words. And the street outside, a boy
                    calling one of our names, or the other, or both.

How could
How would
How on earth should anyone know how
to do this?

Regarding the Woman Lying Naked in the Grass

One more reason to not trust
        where August's hands have been: humidity having its
           frantic way
              with the denim that was, an hour ago, awful
around her thighs. Her dove-feathered behind. All of it green and tolling
        all of it bloomless. Still the vascular smell
                      of red snapper inside the house
              from dinner last night, the windows open
to let in air. Still the well water, cloudy in her porcelain sink, and these
  salt bagels
        not what she ordered. Still those who would tell her
                beauty is something other than what asks
        a moment of adjustment
in the lives of those who see it. The trees doing that Goya thing
                with the colors. Only a world like ours
            would think we could know what to do with it.

The Rules

I don't believe in girlhood. I don't believe
we are ever small, or ever don't know what it is
we shouldn't know. I don't believe thick minutes in July
crept any closer to the ground than on the tennis court
at Hidden Creek Country Club, where sky-browned Tony,
with eyebrows bleached bright from the sun, strapped me
at the end of our lesson into an elastic harness
anchored by the chain-link fence, net running across the court
like a hard spine, my sisters on the other side, and
eyebrows almost on his knees, adult arms around me, taking
    as long as he wanted
to snap the clasps in place. He'd back up, yell
Serve! to my sisters and I ran to them,
slapped backward by its quick yank
at my waist and home later, my middle sister, four years younger
so I guess she was seven, says *Courtney, Tony has a cwush on you*—
    said it
in that lisp of hers we laughed about
two days ago watching home footage, our mother behind the camera
laughing too, our mother like a shapely soda bottle
with lipstick at the rim, our mother who played Patsy Cline so often
that there was my sister, singing *Cway-thee*, eyes nuclear
and luminous, never breaking contact with the camera. We do
    nothing now
but sing it like she did then. Play it in the morning
on our way to summer jobs at the Club, where she flips burgers
by the pool and I bring beer around to golfers

wearing left-handed gloves that hide their wedding rings.
Every time I pass the cabana, my sister's bent over the counter texting
her boyfriend, in a boxy uniform she calls *unsexy
as hell, thank God*, and every time I leave her it's to bend into
the cart to find a Modelo for Mr. Richards who likes
my little shorts, he says, who likes sunflower seeds, spitting
them diagonally between sentences, who calls me best
in the business, says, *we were all talkin 'bout you today, 'bout how
you know the rules so well*, meaning I'm quiet, unlike
Barbara, who wears khaki pants and drives her cart
*like a demon banshee in heat, plowin' right up there when we're
  teein' off,*
and between the 12th and 13th hole I drive the path
along that tennis court where even at eleven I was barely
there, my ribcage the circumference of a Folgers coffee tin
and Tony was lifting my shirt to put his hand
on the harness' angry red marks, asking if it hurt, and no,
I'd say, it feels like nothing, it felt like nothing at all.

Miscarriage

What I remember is how my mother used her entire body
to yank the gear of our red jeep into park, then turned

around in her seat to say she'd *only be a minute; wait quietly*.
She rolled my window down but forgot to close her door

which made the dashboard complain in beeps and bells
and this upset me. Her coffee was left in the holder, hanging

its adult smell over the car like a shadow. She ran
across the grass to where her friend was heaped

on the front steps in a white linen dress, very loose, rumpled
and twisted as bed sheets emptied of arms and legs. I remember

it was the woman who let me wear her wedding ring
whenever I sat on her lap; who'd kiss the top of my head, telling me

the only thing strong enough to cut such a perfect stone
was another just like it. There on the bricks, she shook

so hard I thought that diamond must have cut her. It was the kind
of sob where no real noise comes out,

sputtering only one word—one I'd never heard before:
lucy-lucy-lucy. I didn't know what a *lucy-lucy-lucy* was

but I grew light-headed from its sound. It reminded me
of air slapping against cement, again and again,

on the flower-bothered basketball courts down the street.
It had a rhythm like the rosary or brushing teeth: that quiet,

swishing, frenzied grasp and drag. I won't describe it, I don't want
to describe it. The two sat as hot and damp and helpless

as the rest of July. Its red-rimmed sun. All night the yellow jackets—
in their tiny waists—whirred themselves hoarse with lament.

Fifth Joyful Mystery

At Union Station a woman has lost her child
in the crowd. The concourse is flooded, choked
with hair, and she is drowned, she is drowning, she is about
to drown. Her son's brief body.
His fleshy wrist, his leash

                        cast off, the ringing in her fingerbones,
having made of devotion a kind of cruelty.
      The security guard holds a small red sweater
as though, at once, immaculate
and in flames. The train to Philadelphia

                               calls and no one
hears—she is a volume specific to the pitch
of speechlessness. She is running as if free, meaning, also,
very much alone.
                Who took her child. Who would want
her child. Aren't children terrifying. She thinks so, turning wildly
    in circles, as if chased. The camera phones are out and
aimed: what she is doing now

                      is what the moon does
    when it is held down underwater, by which I mean,
something we haven't words for.

Cardiac

Not so much the architecture as its evidence.
Not its four chambers, high beamed atriums more gothic
than baroque. Not the arteries, hauling blue freight.
Less pomegranate,
more its eight dozen rubies,
                       unhidden if you're good
with a knife. Heart with its headache. With its own set of vowels,
its ratifying pulse:
                 because, because, because.
Bucket of honey heart, fish-naked heart, heart
wrapped fast in the dirty sheets
                       of its body. Heart pinned
and sightless—a fly in cupped hands. Arrhythmic heart,
the extra beats chasing around inside it
like a squirrel. Heart with its phantom limb, its pimples
and headgear. Apiary heart. Spooked-horse heart.
Heart like a pink moon risen high
                 in the chest. Heart
at half-mast. Carton-of-milk heart, that sweats
and sours in the heat. Heart with its spreadsheets
and penniless laugh. Heart ringing
                 off the hook.
A light-rain heart. A rub-some-dirt-on-it
heart. Revving heart, all rotor hum and easy reverse, sparks
gathered in its arms like arrows, turning around

until the body must, too. A come-
no-closer heart. Runaway heart
praying like hell that it's followed. Unknowable,
unlikable heart. It could be anything in there, sealed
as it is, in such a darkness.

Piccola Morte

In 1902 Alessandro Serenelli saw Maria Goretti.

What frightened me most as his body pinned mine
against the porch stairs that same way

I opened jam jars—anchoring the glass between my skirt
and the counter—was how Alex had almost no eyelashes,

just a trace of ash collected at the lids, and how
left-over light was dripping off the leaves like sweat

down the muzzle of a horse, and on the beam above us
a wren had made its nest from the bones and feathers

of another bird, so I was lost a moment, counting
terrible things of its arteries and how they must

have spilled like black seeds from the wind's pockets,
and how it wasn't beautiful, this noise of skin

breaking that made the cows put their soft heads
on the ground, made a mess like bathwater and he stood

in it, stood later to recall *it was like pounding corn–drilling holes
in a log–churning cream to butter*, and I guess

an hour before, I'd have said "forgiveness" was a thing
that helped you sleep at night, but what frightened me

was "forgiveness" as suddenly the thing to give quickly
and for others: my mother who would find her child

and not recognize her (mistaken for an animal
abandoned at the door), not until she saw my signs

of fight: elbows ribboned from pulling myself
across the floor, until she'd found all ten torn crescents

of my fingernails, fishing them, personally, from his hair.

*You were one of them: one of his girls
against his desk
assuming what he did to you
was love.*

Annunciation

Before he began to motion
with his hands, molting, almost: flinging

the news from his limbs
like black feathers. Before something crawled

inside me, as if with life. Before he appeared
different to me, somehow, the way a book might

for having read it, though neither of us
equipped with sounds taut enough to call

this anything—my body rioting
like parts of a chandelier

as it hits the ground. Before he told me
that he'd told me what he'd never

told anyone—telling it with the exact aim
of having practiced at the mirror

when alone, when absolutely
alone, or before the difference between a pulse

and its rippling meant something
between us, between throatsore and gumsore,

between stopping a thing inside myself,
and a stopping of the thing itself. Before

his sentences began, and they began
constantly, meaning he kept reaching toward me,

meaning maybe my stillness was a kind of instinct
for it, like that of a horse

stepping into its harness, and you could
call it that, and he did.

Wax Wings

Suspecting, even then, that the tent
his bones made—pitched
                    above me—was mostly
   just that. Quick-stitched distance. The visible seams
of a body my own seemed anxious to mistake
   for love—for *want*,
        as if the craving for shadow. A canvassed stretch of human
to hide beneath. Suspecting, even now, the sun
                  as some vision of god: with no end
                          to its being alone.

Sinfonietta

I knew him three days in San Francisco
four years ago, but it's still only
recklessness and a sort of self-indulgence
that keeps me sticking myself with these shards
of a few seconds, recalling the angle
of the chin—of total concentration—
as he unhooked and pulled his watch
off his wrist with its special double clasp
that let his large hand through.
The street we stood on widened
To the width of his palm. It was obvious
He was the wrong size for that city.
It made me want to touch him and I didn't.

Pink Moon

The mosquito lands, and my neck is red
with its own blood. This season takes

no prisoners. A summer boy is dragging
his clumsy love to me like he'd pull a beach chair

across searing sand. That stuff heats up—and so
does he. He tells me that we both have beating hearts

and should conduct ourselves accordingly.
To make his point he stands at my door. Unbuttons

the first four holes of his shirt. A slow unfastening
that makes the birds branched above us start

to sweat, their feathers emerald-wet as mallards.
Even the moon turns pink, and moves to hide her eyes

behind a cloud. He's trembling. Beneath his opened
collar, I can see that heart banging its purple fist

against his skin—
thin vellum of a deep and howling drum.

Letter to His Wife

You don't know me, nor clearly
                much know him—though at night
           you let his legs entangle yours:
                    naked, maybe; the thermostat adjusted
    to a temperature you've both agreed
feels right after years

    of co-deciding, the sheets you're twisted in
               cleaned with a mutually agreed upon
        detergent, a grocery list for paper towels
and tortillas, the brand
            with the woman, pinned

to the refrigerator
        to pick up on his way home
      from office hours. Hours

some of his students call otherwise. Maybe now
        you turn him up

                  and down, like lipstick in a tube, thinking
that he's changed. Maybe one student

took her keys off a Pottery Barn cast-iron 6-hook fixture
           opened a door and filled her garage
                 with carbon monoxide. The rest of us left
      to plant her favorite flowers. *Impatiens.* Also known

as *Touch-Me-Not*s. My mother always thought that it's pronounced
   Impatience,
                      and I like that so much more.
              I am a person who grew to know
                      what measure of water

hydrangeas thirst for in the last days
                of July; what a spud wrench can be used for;
    what the phrase *beg the question*
                          really means. But also, what
your husband's aftershave smells of; what his reasons are
              for keeping his office at 61 degrees.

   How it feels to be at the wrong end
               of the cruel strength of his hands. What sort of man
is he to you. What color are your children's eyes.
                    What to hope for, or if.

Refrain of Him Singing Songs with Her about Us

Says he doesn't love her but needs her
    voice for his own
        to make sense. To make music.

Little Dogs

Even now, the danger is forgetting how it matters—
          matters he's become a story you tell yourself,
              or rather, retell,
     which is to say, less the telling, and more, ever,
                  an ache in its direction: a story
he stands rained on ready to hear, and you want to tell it
          without having any part in it, and he can smell it
on you, this shift from pheromones to a guilt
            that daubed its thin perfume behind the ears.
Insufficient, the merely irresistible. His eyes—the distant towns
  and small cities
            of your body, unlit; *Let's not   Let's not*
    a stammering extremely sure
you have no idea what it is you don't want, the saltiness
           of words of love and the instinct not to,
                    of what beats
and is beaten, which is to say, the heart, which says, as usual,
we have ourselves a problem. Slumped and buttoned, quiet
                as sacks of meat. Don't look at me
like that, all shadow-bitten, like one of those little dogs
              a person can make of his hands.

*My foreign way of folding
his shirts, so different
than how he'd learned
from his mother.*

Eyelash

It was surely *he* who was in peril,
   looking down at her
across his thick lower lashes

as if leaned, reckless, over the bars
   of a balcony. Control was hers,
and her feet, she told herself, were firm

upon the ground. But how to stay
   that way, with night dropping around them
in ripened swoons, like soft pears

off a tree. The wiry thighs of the crickets
   had begun to creak
and roses were discarding their humid petals,

pooled as fabric at their feet.
   He was six foot six, with lips an altitude
completely out of reach. She'd need to climb,

or worse, jump. But jumping
   was out of the question. Evening presumed
to know what was best, and intervened:

shaking out its black blanket of fireflies
   so they could lie beneath it
shoulder to shoulder in the grass. She'd never

seen such lashes up so close—
    hand-stitched to his boyish face,
as though each had been pulled out

then carefully sewn back on. It was clear he
    could teach her something
about pain. Clearer still, her sudden yearn for it.

How to Make Love in a Poem

Best to forget about loyalty
to facts. Write in first person
or risk sounding like a voyeuristic creep. Take the demure
and tousle its hair: every time the word "bedpost"
would appear, change it to "fencepost," and assume
a ragged tone, a jaded voice suggesting
you've done this before, thus wearily
well-equipped to comment
on the subject. Don't mention the moon being out
and in full. No one will believe you,
nor want to. Still others may interpret it
as pun. Say instead that there was no moon
at all, or, if you *must* have moonlight, make it red
and emitted from no apparent
source. The color white has no place
in your poem. It's late and the two of you
have been drinking—not a lot—just enough
to describe the few bright stars as bubbles in champagne
and to remark that he held onto your wrist
as though clasping a wine bottle by its neck.
Say the wind was out, and your hands
shook the entire time
like uppermost leaves on the trees.
And though the deed be set outdoors,
avoid any mention of the nest of cardinals
nearby. Their chirps suggest a baby, which is not
the direction you want your poem to go; it wrecks

the mood, which by this point should
be turning pretty sexy. Set aside the cardinals
but keep an open mind to crows, perhaps a nest
of them hatching noisily, as they do,
tearing from their shells into the night's
purple shadow. (As a rule, any time
a hue as counter-intuitive
as "purple shadow" makes an appearance,
it hints to sensations that cannot be explained.)
Keep the presence of animals
to a minimum. Allow an exception for the lone
ginger horse who has begrudgingly shared
his pasture. After his ruddy color, the two of you
give him a name—say, Pineapple. Avoid mentioning Pineapple's
wide stance and strong jaw—he should not
seem like a metaphor for your lover. Rather, a sort
of guardian angel—watching, wondering, winnowing.
All those airy "W" sounds to get the point across.
Do not resort to images of flowers
unless to compare pillowed hydrangeas to the scent
and rustle of his blue jeans. At highest moments
of sweetness, break off for a bit—
a circuitous discourse on your childhood, its lost
innocence, via descriptions of herbs and spices.
Jasmine, lavender, paprika. The reader
will lean forward, as if smelling something
that is being slowly drawn away. Should you ever
use the word "heaven," use it only
to remark that it is nowhere. Just the world

breathing heavily in your ear. Suggest you might
have cried out when he touched you with his
life. Describe your insides as audible;
that when the distant thunder purred
he assumed it was your heart. At this point, shift the poem
to a clumsy lineation that suggests the *type*
of lovemaking. If the reader is uncomfortable
and in slight pain, you're doing your job. The final
few lines would be a good place to bring back
that carrot-colored horse. Return to it
when your reader least wants you to. End on a note
of indecision with a few observations
that Beauty is the Space across which Desire reaches.
Take the lover by his hand and back
across the field to wherever it was you came from,
stopping only, and suddenly, to whisper at his neck
Pineapple, Pineapple, Pineapple.

Nocturne in What Now Feels Like a Very Silly Dress

Tonight there are no taxis
        in Harlem, and the moon is somewhere,
                      mustering itself the way a man does
to take himself to someone else.
You know this night. The one so large you can stand full height
inside it, your eyes blade-level
   with its throat. And this street, you know it too: busy intersection
where you speak a little louder to be heard
                      above the blood inside you, gunning
two directions like traffic down a bridge. The taxi, if you could
   find one,
is for only you, though he is standing here—
        because though he's just left you, he won't leave you
until he's seen you safely
     on your way—the good-guy, the gentleman, fearing nothing
so much, as appearing *not* to be. He has to think a little louder
   to be heard
above these speeches corked
        inside him, the ones he knows you wouldn't listen to
in a way he would enjoy. He has watched you die
before. His silence, which is a doorlessness
the street comes, also, to resemble. His hands half-hidden
                        in his shirt sleeves, like a boy.

Cartography

You've tried, you really have, you're saying
to your buddies at the bar, but there really is
no better way of describing her person
than as a book of maps pointing the direction
of your own. And you're sorry, really—well, a little
sorry—that it's ended this way, this compass
wheeling into all directions, those thighs
you gave yourself to, thought you'd do something
interesting with, but there you were,
tongue climbing the latitudes
of her body, thinking all the while mostly
of yourself: how those stories about her family
made you feel; that her irises' foreign color
left you questioning your personal
and professional decisions. Her short arms
taught you yours are long; that your hair
looks best when a girl's hands misbehave
inside it; that your fear of lightning
is normal—*it's fine, it's really fine*—and for all
of that, you owe her, you do, though you doubt
by now, she'd take it—anything—from
you, a week since your name in her mouth
has done cold, glossy things
to both your bodies. *Do your impression
of her again*—someone's saying—*but wait
till I get back*, hikes the belt loops
of his Levi's, brings another pitcher from the bar,

the beer disappearing like whole people do
into desire, and you're lit with it, alive
and pulling at the air, entertaining them with how
her door was stuck just after you'd told her—
how she couldn't get it open,
shoulder thrown against it, your mock-wild face
imitating her own's attempt *not* to be,
and they're howling now, because it's funny.
They stack their cups like many glassy pieces
of an argument. Lie down with us
in our lives, they say, There is always more
of the world, they say, She is meaner now, and
more beautiful.

At Their Wedding

To see the way he looks at her
        is to learn something
of the sweet agony

of looking at the one you love.
        It is to watch a woman being memorized
the way a sunrise is

by a painter going blind:
        anguish and reverence and hunger.
Inside of him, the heart

is snapping its ropes
        to lean away from his own body
toward hers, like a kiss.

To watch him watch her
        is to watch devotion define itself: speak
her name and his face awakens

as if recognizing his own.
        And to see the way she watches him
is to witness a woman's face

emitting light like a holy thing.
        Both aglow from the look she is given,
and glowing with the look

that she gives. Joy travels from her in waves,
> like rings across the surface of water.

At her shine, those around her

turn their heads at once,
> as any wide-eyed school of fish.

Hers is a look that lights

whatever twilight she enters—
> at night when windows pray,

if they do pray, each begs to be lit like this.

Skin and Other Weapons

You worry me, jumping out the shower
so quickly, contrails of soap
in your wake to where I've fallen, smallest splinter
of Tennessee pine in my foot, bit of lightning
through this body you sweep up to set down on the rim
of the tub, shampoo suds like slow glaciers
down your neck, your ears, your wet lashes
gathered into spears, turning my foot
over in your hands: twenty-six bones like a loose bundle
of sticks, the underside so dirty I'd never
in my right mind let you see—debris picked up
off the kitchen floor the way rooms stay
a while on your skin; the way this morning
we broke eggs against the stove to watch them
shiver in the pan, the coffee grinder's two blades
spinning half an inch apart as if afraid
of wounding each other. Your body goosebumped
tending mine, clothes a heap in the hall, socks
balled up at the bathroom door, my stray blondes
laced into their soles as if stitching
me to you, and you holding out your hand
for the sterilized pin as if to say give me something
to hurt you with, and I do, head thrown back
like watching the surgery channel when a doctor,
mid-incision, tells the camera that in cases
such as these, the best way to the heart
is through the spine. How you flinch

whenever I do, at the wrong angle tenderness
sometimes gets a hold of, asking—is it here, or here,
or here. Shrapnel too small
to claim a weight, or color, or shape. How little
love is. How worth everything.

How such evil still exists is less
A question than a water glass I want to throw
Against the wall.

Inventory of Half-Burnt Offerings

We're late because according to Virginia State law
the intersection of West Ox
& Bennett Road is only two deaths away
from the installation of a traffic light—great news
but no one's volunteering: the stop sign line
stretching cautious for a mile, a single car gingering
forward at a time. My foot on the brake,
we practiced saying eight different options
for hello. Where the inflections go. To pronounce
her name with eye contact. With her shoulders
straight back, like Pocahontas—her favorite
Disney princess. To send her arm out like a paper boat
in the other direction. That *Yes*, I promised, *they will
offer their hand too*. It's easy to say true things
without feeling any truth in them. Her kid-size
equestrian boots dirtying the dashboard, both hands
upwards on her lap as if a catalogue
of gestures for the frequently speechless, and by now
we're *so* late the horses at her therapeutic riding class
were led already from the stable—Lucinda, Tess,
and Spirit fronting the pack. The noise of nails
in their feet. The puckered six-inch scars
guttering their flanks, gashes that look worse
in person than they did in the daily paper. I read
they caught the boy who knifed them—who crept
into the barn that night, all of us left wondering
what pain is for. Not the dramatic part, the sound

of horse-skin breaking, reddening
the hay. I mean its afterache: my sister's face
as she's legged-up to the saddle. Her woundedness
imagining theirs. Seconds before, she walked up
to the teacher in her sweet, robotic way. Gave her hand
like we'd rehearsed it, then joined the others
in the class. If grace could be
defined it'd be a very quiet phrase. All that braided
hair. The burdens on their backs. Each body
half on fire, the other half in flame.

Fabric

Today I wait in line at Kroger behind a boy
              wearing a white cotton t-shirt, his backbones
       slim—track-runner-taut—the way yours were,
                          my basket foolish with hummus
           and clementines and I think that if you'd made it
      to twenty-five they're how yours would look
    too, and I'm breathing
at his neck, at the luxury
           of his shoulder blades and I'm jealous of him
                for you: how this boy with hands in his pockets
was yoked to the morning
   and pulled along. How his t-shirt turns him into the canvas
                     of any sun-stunned Saturday—
       how all he has to do is stand here and he's a palette
bleached by noon, stained gold
        in the moonlight, or reddened with dawn. How the day
      rubs itself off on him, unasked.
Beauty is what the memory never abandons: a stretch of fabric,
        sunning itself across your shoulders. Supine horizon,
wanting only, and always, more light.

Black Licorice

I was standing in an elevator on Wednesday trying
to remember if I was headed up or down. I'd been in there
for a while and had lost track of the usual sensations
that help a guy know if he is plummeting or ascending.
A woman and her cat-faced son were in there too.
After the kid pretended to walk into the walls for a while,
he lit the reddish button for the 15th floor, holding it down
with his finger. "I don't know what to do with him
anymore," the woman said to her cell phone. "This morning
they sent him home for putting raccoon urine on the doorknobs
of the teachers' lounge. It smelled like black licorice
and wouldn't wash off. The entire faculty taught with their hands
in plastic bags." I was listening closely to her conversation,
keeping the elbows of the small convict in clear view.
I felt naked and defenseless. He knew I was watching, and turned
his head slowly to look at me. His eyes pulled all the air in the lift
toward him like quicksand. "We don't even live near raccoons,
Bill, and I think it's time to try military school."
The boy brought his eyes to slits and watched me like a reptile.
By now I didn't care where I was going, so long as I stayed
off the 15th floor. It was hot as blazes in that elevator,
but he wouldn't look away, wouldn't take
his cake-colored finger off that single, bloodshot key.

Errata

After Chelsea Wagenaar

Replace car with smoke rising

Where it says nearness read the body's jar of hours

and because capital letters bring along a promise of permanence
remove them altogether

When it says mother follow it with yoked
to the morning and pulled along

In the two lines it says sons read son and wherever Charlottesville
   is mentioned or alluded to read
      black blanket of fireflies or half-flooded road across the field

When the poem asks for more light honor its request

In place of cotton list the names of bones in his back
thoracic lumbar sacral there were thirty-three and each more
   useful than the last

When a word is underlined read hair and at hair read dark eyes
of a horse opening

Anywhere it says home read bloodload
read lemons yellowing his brother still standing at the door

Elegy at Middle River

It's an hour before noon, and Amtrak train no. 56 rips a path
through the rain outside Baltimore,
its speed screamed across the iron-black bones
of the track, our train now stopping in the woods,
no platform, and I pull Al Green
out of my ears to a car completely hushed. We wait,
wait longer, till the intercom stirs; says
nothing. Someone folds gum into his mouth and chews.
An older couple up ahead is peeling the skin
off dark plums. Across the aisle a little girl's feet dangle
inches from a slippery floor scummy from people's shoes,
holding a water-filled bag of goldfish to her face
like a hungry cat. Her mother looks over, smiles,
covers her daughter's ears, explains, *we hit something,
probably a deer*, so low she only mouths it,
and we watch another train worker pass
beneath the windows, his hair gathered and curled
in the rain. A man comes back from the train café,
hands his wife her tea, tells her the conductor's locked
himself in the restroom, won't come out,
and for the next two hours no one
speaks a word. Sometimes an arm
pulled through a sleeve, skin surfacing for air.
Sometimes the gravel's gray teeth
crunched under service men's boots. Sometimes a moan
from the dumb weight of the engine—a beast stilled
by what is pinioned beneath it. The little girl

opens her bag of fish, and pushes half of her sandwich,
crusts cut off by her mother, into the water, and outside
a dog barks at nothing, a siren, and a worker's found a phone,
holding it out like it's burning his hand, and the little girl
tosses the sopped bread into the aisle, one of her fish
flopping out with it and I listen to its wetted slap,
watch it flail, rose-gold and nothing's getting better,
and we know it.

It's You I Like

My sister spins her wine glass by its stem
searching for adult versions of the childproof words
she speaks in every day. How the alarm for an active shooter drill
sounded different than the one they use for fires,
ringing out at school this morning like European sirens
in an Anne Frank movie, her first graders
looking up from phonics workbooks to watch her
lock their windows down, shut the blinds
to daylilies, tiger-striped and lazy on the playground,
cover the classroom's frosted door with black cotton
like mirrors when in mourning. How she squeezed
her twenty-four kids into the supply closet—bodies
small enough to somehow fit, taught to squat down low
against the floor. How "practice" and "preparation" are not
the same, exactly, though they can seem so—fear
speaking its own language in each child: whimpers
from Eloise crouching at the back; Jack's eyes wide
as if a punishment his fault; a ball of wetted underwear
hidden in Manishka's fist, and James knows everyone
is scared so he has asked to sing
the Mister Rogers song, and though it broke the rules
my sister let them, just this once and only
at a whisper, let them sing—*It's you I like, not the things you wear,
not the way you do your hair, but it's you I like*—James, who
told her once, "anticipation is the sincerest form
of affection," big words, but not for James, who learned it
in Korean too; who claps erasers without ever

being asked, and starts his day before the bell
with pushups in the middle of the aisle; who got in trouble
last week with Salvatore, snickering at cartoon illustrations
of Princess Jasmine's cleavage, the Aladdin book
now confiscated for a while—*the way you are right now,*
the way down deep inside you; not the things
that hide you—twenty-four children huddled behind a door
covered on the other side by maps of the Earth in quilted color
to teach them that if you look for the world
you can find it—*but it's you I like, every part of you—your skin,*
your eyes, your feelings, whether old or new—and the principal
walks the hallway, rattling doorknobs, testing the locks, my sister
certain at its sound that she would use the wrench
and can of wasp spray hidden in her file cabinet
to protect them if she could, her belief in evil not yet taken,
entirely, by her faith that she can ward
it all away—*I hope that you remember even when*
you're feeling blue—their heads popping up
from the ground to point around to each other
the way my sister taught—*that it's you I like,*
it's you yourself, it's you—a seasick silence at its finish, and James
begins the song again, the others follow; quiet little choir
in the almost-total dark, faces pressed against the floor,
singing to some goodness in our world.

*The light has yet to notice it's been torn
in half behind her. Her aloneness never so willing
or sudden or soft.*

A NOTE FROM WILL ANDERSON, COURTNEY'S HUSBAND

I am generally a cynical person. I don't believe in fate or karma, and especially not the clichéd trope where meeting one person changes everything. But in solitary moments, when I'm alone and no one is around to call me out on my hypocrisy, I allow myself one exception to this rule:

I can say with full, unflinching certainty that my entire life changed the day I met Courtney Kampa.

We met on a Monday in the fall of 2006, on the Lawn at the University of Virginia. I was just starting my third year and she was a first year. I heard an unfamiliar voice yell out my name and looked up to find a blond, fair-skinned, barefoot girl skipping across the grass toward me. She was wearing a white skirt, a white blouse, and was the most gorgeous person I'd ever seen.

I don't remember what we talked about that day, but I learned that Courtney knew my name because we had mutual friends. That first conversation on the quad led to seven years of friendship, four years of dating, and five years of marriage. But that wasn't just the day I met my soulmate and best friend; it was the moment that I first got a glimpse into the incredible mind of a generational talent.

Now, you should know that I've never been a fan of poetry. (See aforementioned cynicism.) It wasn't that I wasn't a natural reader—

I've been obsessed with sci-fi and historical fiction for as long as I can remember. And as a musician, the limitations of the form felt familiar to me. I was constantly thinking about the economy of language, how to make emotionally resonant statements in just a few words. So why couldn't I be bothered to remember the name of a single poet? Why didn't I feel anything when I read "the greats"? Why did poetry feel like a foreign language that, no matter how many hours I spent with it, slipped through my fingers?

Then, suddenly, there was Courtney—unlatching a trapdoor and letting down a rope ladder, welcoming me into her most precious and favorite space. She quieted my resistance and showed me not only why poetry is worth loving, but why it is worth getting *excited* over. And I wasn't the only one; converting readers was one of her greatest joys. She believed that, if she sat with someone for an hour, she could go home and write a poem they would like. And usually, she was right.

Because, while Courtney's writing was always layered and insightful and funny, the real brilliance of her work was its accessibility. She didn't write for other poets—or even, really, for herself. She wrote for the teenage girls in the freshman writing classes she taught, who began the semester thinking poetry was pretentious, dull, and insufferably high-minded and ended the semester hungry for more.

Every word Courtney put on paper was a challenge to those who'd written off poetry as a form for someone else. She asked her readers to put aside the usual sterile, academic lens through which they were taught to read poetry, and encouraged them to *delight* in the meter, syllables, and images, and in every solitary word. She wanted you not only to understand a poem, but also to cherish it.

To that end, Courtney obsessed over every line break, every word choice, every punctuation mark, wanting to be sure there was never a wasted moment. And she knew that worthwhile creative work took time. She'd spend weeks trying to find her way into an idea she'd been stewing on, and I'd hear her scream from across the house when she cracked it. She dedicated herself to developing her voice and was self-aware enough to know when a poem wasn't right—not because it wasn't "good," but because it didn't yet sound like *her*. For Courtney, the value of writing was in the act of creation itself. She was enamored with the process, the deliberate care it took to place one word next to another, the responsibility of creating an entire world just to share one quiet part of yourself with another person.

My life changed again on November 14, 2022, when Courtney passed away suddenly in her sleep. She was thirty-five years old.

In the days after she died, I could barely think, lost in what Joan Didion calls the swirling "vortex of grief." But amid the turmoil, my mind kept returning to a conversation we'd had a few weeks earlier—about her desire to publish more of her poems and her ambition to reach readers where they are.

Like many other poets before her, Courtney won't see the legacy of her work. And of course, I wish "her time" had come while she was still here to witness it herself. But, in her absence, I hope this book can invite readers into the same warm and welcoming clubhouse that Courtney built for me so many years ago. Nothing will make up for the fact that we've been robbed of a lifetime of her brilliance, art, kindness, and love, but if this collection can succeed at sharing her greatest passion with the world, I'm confident that her poetry will change readers' lives just as much as meeting that shoeless, beatific vision in white changed mine.

NOTES

"Ars Balletica" references G. K. Chesterton's famous lines "Angels fly because they take themselves lightly" (from *Orthodoxy*) and "The Christian ideal has not been tried and found wanting. It has been difficult; and left untried" (from *What's Wrong with the World*).

The title of "Fifth Joyful Mystery" references a decade of the Catholic rosary, the story of the "Finding in the Temple," when Mary loses her son, Jesus.

ACKNOWLEDGMENTS

FROM WILL

Thank you to Dana Murphy at Trellis for your endless patience and hard work in making this book a reality, and for being an incredible champion of Courtney and her life's work.

To Catherine Pond and Taneum Bambrick for being such amazing friends to Courtney and helping her voice be heard with your choice of poems.

To Tessa James, for taking a chance on this book and recognizing Courtney's vision and passion for poetry. And to Sharyn Rosenblum, Amelia Wood, Amanda Hong, Elina Cohen, Yeon Kim, and the rest of the team at William Morrow.

To Lauren McKinney at Foundations Management, David Kostiner and the team at Counsell LLP, and Fabian Munoz.

To New Issues Poetry & Prose for publishing Courtney's first collection of poems, *Our Lady of Not Asking Why*.

FROM COURTNEY, REPRINTED FROM HER COLLECTION *OUR LADY OF NOT ASKING WHY*

To my parents Joseph and Kathleen, who on any given Wednesday teach me more about love and sacrifice than poems ever could. And to my sisters Keenan, Meggie, and Grace, whose fingerprints are all over everything I do.

To William Anderson, my long-loved and even-longer-adored.

To my teachers at the University of Virginia and Columbia University, particularly Lisa Russ Spaar, my poetry mama and unflagging example of what true care for one's students looks like. Thank you to the wild minds and soft hearts of Timothy Donnelly, Lucie Brock-Broido, Mark Strand, John Casteen, Timothy Green, Gregory Orr, Rita Dove, David Keplinger, Amy Lemmon, and Patrick Knisley.

To the most talented writers in my life, Chelsea Wagenaar and Catherine Pond. To my first poetry ally and backyard-confidant, Luke Cumberland, and my favorite wolf Grant Rosson; to the constant kindness of Mark Wagenaar and C. Russel Price. To John Fenlon Hogan, always my better and smarter set of eyes, and to my graduate school sweethearts Jay Deshpande, Hilary Vaughn Dobel, Marina Blitshteyn, and Austen Rosenfeld.

To the women who impact my life in more ways than they know—Logan Lambert, Missy Tacey Brooks, Laura LaMonica, Allison Baughman, and Nicole Caruso. To my Bella. And to Amy and Mark Anderson, who have become my second home.

To passed loved ones, whose memories I hope are honored in the small stories held within these pages: Donald Louise Hanrahan, John Kotaro Barnes, and Gregory Iarrobino.

Finally, to the unfathomable generosity of the Elizabeth George Foundation, who took a chance on a twenty-three-year-old girl from Virginia. Without that grant, this book probably would not have made it into your hands.

Thank you to the editors of the following publications in which many of these poems, often in earlier forms, first appeared:

Boston Review: "Annunciation"

Colorado Review: "Ars Balletica"

Drunken Boat: "Cartography"

H.O.W. Journal: "Saint Anthony and the Jarflies"

h_ng_m_n: "Wax Wings"

The Journal: "Inventory of Half-Burnt Offerings"

Leveler: "Driving into the Lilacs"

Missouri Review: "Replica"

New England Review: "Cardiac"

Philadelphia Stories: "The Rules"

Poets & Writers Magazine: "Fifth Joyful Mystery"

Rattle: "Miscarriage," "Self-Portrait by Someone Else," "Baby Love," "Nocturne in What Now Feels Like a Very Silly Dress"

Salmagundi: "Skin and Other Weapons"

Two Peach: "Short Essay at the Sink"

"Fifth Joyful Mystery" won the 2011 Amy Award through *Poets & Writers Magazine*.

ABOUT THE AUTHOR

COURTNEY KAMPA held a BA in creative writing from the University of Virginia and an MFA from Columbia University, where she won the David Craig Austin Memorial Award for Outstanding Thesis. A 2016 Ruth Lilly finalist and winner of the 2014 Rattle Poetry Prize Readers' Choice Award, she was awarded a Wallace Stegner Fellowship at Stanford University in 2017. Courtney taught at the Fashion Institute of Technology, Belmont University, and Lipscomb University, and she received awards and distinctions from *Best New Poets*, *The Atlantic*, *Poets & Writers Magazine*, and *North American Review*. Her work has been published in *Boston Review*, *TriQuarterly*, *The Journal*, *The National Poetry Review*, *Missouri Review*, *New England Review*, and elsewhere. She passed away in 2022.